Dr. Dee Dee Dynamo's

Mission to Pluto

By Oneeka Williams, M.D.
Illustrated by Valerie Bouthyette

PRT0713B
Library of Congress Control Number: 2012953742
Printed in the United States
ISBN-13: 9781620861851
ISBN-10: 1620861852
www.mascotbooks.com

To my grandmothers, Doris and Audrey,
upon whose shoulders I stand.

Thank you to my husband, Charles,
my son, Mark, my parents,
and extended family
for believing in my dream.

Thank you to my sister friends
who supported me on this journey.

Zzzzzzzzzzzzzzzzzzzzzzzzzzzzip!

Dr. Dee Dee Dynamo zooms out of her bedroom window. She starts her day by flying over the gleaming sandy beaches and sparkling seawater surrounding the Island of Positivity. She does a double somersault over her cousin and best friend Lukas' house and returns home.

As she circles over her lush and colorful yard, she greets her grandfather. "Good morning, Granddad Willy."

"Good morning, dearie. Are you getting ready for a new surgical mission?"

"I'm CHARGED UP and READY TO GO!"

Dr. Dee Dee is super excited and bursting with energy. She is a girl surgeon with special powers and she loves to operate. She can hardly wait for her next mission. Dr. Dee Dee Dynamo is always ready to use her surgical instruments to fix anything. Her fingertips are actually tingling! They are tingling not only from excitement, but also because Dr. Dee Dee's power comes from electrical energy.

Kyle the Koala Bear opens one eye as Dr. Dee Dee flies back into her bedroom. Kyle is Dr. Dee Dee's very irritable assistant. He loves to eat, sleep, and sort eucalyptus leaves as he looks for the perfect ones to eat.

His friend, Gordon the Gullible Globe, sits quietly on the nightstand. Gordon has the most sensitive ears in the universe and can hear even the tiniest cry of distress.

"Good morning. Rise and shine!" Dr. Dee Dee greets cheerfully.

Kyle grunts while Gordon beams.

Dr. Dee Dee is famished after her morning flight. She darts into the kitchen where Grandma B is preparing her famous, yummy breakfast.

Grandma B always says to her, "You may have lots of electrical energy, but a healthy breakfast will add a power boost to your roost!"

Dr. Dee Dee's two biggest fans, Mommy and Daddy Dynamo, are setting the table.

"Good morning, my favorite parents!"

"Good morning, Dee Dee!" they reply in unison.

Daddy Dynamo is an Electrical Engineer and he remembers not being able to take his eyes off of Dr. Dee Dee's hands when she was born. They were literally glowing. Every day, he tells Dr. Dee Dee that she has the most gifted hands in the universe and that not even the sky is her limit!

He built the Charger Family from batteries so that she could plug in to them for her energy and he also built the watch, Wyndee, who measures Dr. Dee Dee's power.

Mommy Dynamo, a science teacher, enjoys telling the story of the moment she knew that Dr. Dee Dee had special powers. She had walked into Dr. Dee Dee's nursery and watched in amazement as Dr. Dee Dee flew out of her crib, picked up a baby bird that had fallen out of its nest, and used her rattle and bib to fix the bird's broken wing.

No one understands how Dr. Dee Dee got these supernatural abilities, but Dr. Dee Dee believes that something happened during a school science experiment while she was still in her mommy's tummy.

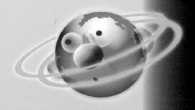

Dr. Dee Dee and Lukas, who slept over, are the first ones
to sit at the breakfast table.
As she waits, Dr. Dee Dee chants with exuberance:

I'm Dr. Dee Dee Dynamo,
Super Surgeon ON THE GO!
My hands were made to heal.
I cut, I sew, I tie with zeal;
No problem is too big or small,
Dr. Dee Dee Dynamo can tackle them all!

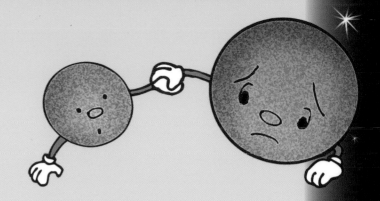

WAHOO, WAHOO, WAHOO!

A loud piercing noise rings through the air.

Lukas jumps and almost falls out of his chair. "Holymackarolee, what in the world?!" he exclaims.

Dr. Dee Dee rushes into her bedroom. Gordon is spinning frantically, screeching loudly and flashing his blue lights.

"What is it, Gordon?" Dr. Dee Dee asks.

"Pluto is having a major meltdown and needs our help!" replies Gordon.

Kyle grumbles, "Why would Pluto be having a meltdown?"

Gordon replies, "He is really sad that he is no longer a planet."

Kyle mutters under his breath, "Did he just wake up and smell the Milky Way? He was downgraded years ago."

"I heard that, Kyle!" chides Dr. Dee Dee gently. "We will help Pluto become a planet again!"

"Oh boy, can I come?" asks Lukas.

"Definitely!" Dr. Dee Dee replies.

She pushes Wyndee's 'ALERT' button, which sends the signal to her team that it's time for a new mission. Her braids crackle as she zips outside to her workroom.

"Be careful. We will be waiting for you," says Mommy Dynamo.

"Keep an eye on Wyndee so you don't run out of energy!" cautions Daddy Dynamo.

As Dr. Dee Dee enters the workroom, Freeda the Flying Ambulance is waiting with doors wide open. She delights in whisking the team anywhere in the universe.

"Team, fasten your seat belts and let's go!" commands Dr. Dee Dee.

Kyle opens Marky Medicine Bag and checks that Slicey Scalpel, Nellie Needleholder, Suzy Suture, Raoul the Retractor, and Simon Scissors are ready. They are Dr. Dee Dee's faithful instruments. Slicey is razor sharp and loves to cut. Nellie and Suzy work together to sew and Raoul keeps the incisions open while Dr. Dee Dee is working.

"Why are we going on this mission, Dr. Dee Dee?" Kyle grunts. "There is no way that you can change Pluto's status."

"I BELIEVE that I can," says Dr. Dee Dee with determination.

"I can't wait to see how you are going to pull this off," mutters Kyle.

Dr. Dee Dee instructs the flying ambulance, "Set GPS for Pluto, the small icy, dwarf planet that is farthest away from the Sun."

"GPS set, Dr. Dee Dee," Freeda replies. She guns her engines and blasts off!

"This is so strange!" remarks Lukas. "How can Pluto be a planet one day and a dwarf planet the next?"

Dr. Dee Dee explains, "To be a planet, a body must do three things: orbit the Sun, maintain its spherical shape, and keep its orbit free of other objects like rocks, dust, and space debris. Pluto could not clear his orbit, so he was downgraded from a planet to a dwarf planet."

"How does a planet keep its orbit clear?" wonders Lukas.

"By using its gravitational force to either suck the objects into the planet or push them away," responds Dr. Dee Dee.

Elliptical Orbit

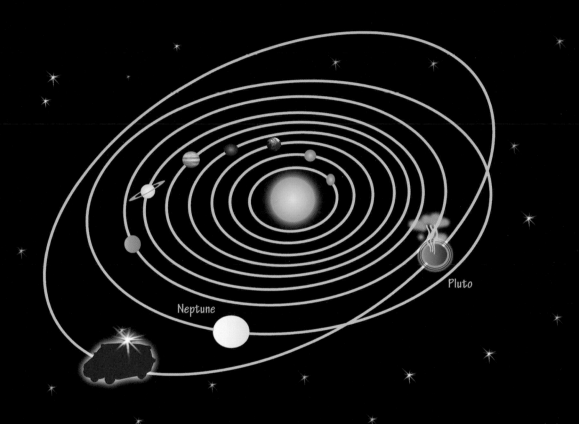

Neptune

Pluto

Meanwhile, Freeda seems to be lost. Dr. Dee Dee peers outside and sees Neptune. "What's the matter, Freeda?" she asks.

"The GPS can't seem to find Pluto. He's supposed to be farther away from the Sun than Neptune, but there's nothing here."

"That's understandable, Freeda. Pluto's orbit is an ellipse so sometimes Pluto is closer to the Sun than Neptune and sometimes he is farther away."

"Thanks, Dr. Dee Dee, that explains the problem!" says Freeda. "Resetting GPS for a small, icy, dwarf planet with an elliptical orbit."

"And also look out for Pluto's moon," adds Dr. Dee Dee.

"This could take forever," complains Kyle.

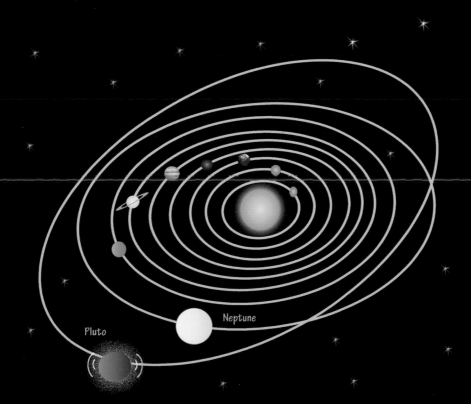

Pluto

Neptune

"There's Pluto, Dr. Dee Dee! Rocky, icy, dwarf planet with an elliptical orbit and a moon," says Freeda.

Dr. Dee Dee and Kyle look outside at the same time. Kyle snorts. "That's not Pluto," he says in disgust.

"What is a dwarf planet anyway?" wonders Lukas.

Dr. Dee Dee explains, "They are bodies that orbit the Sun, are round, and are not a moon or satellite of any other planet."

"Sounds like a planet to me," Lukas responds.

"Tee hee hee," giggles Dr. Dee Dee. "It kind of does! The difference is that a dwarf planet cannot keep its orbit clear of space clutter."

"Yikes, they have messy orbits! Just like my bedroom!" laughs Lukas.

"Freeda, let's keep moving," says Dr. Dee Dee. "Pluto is now closer to the Sun than Neptune so the surface will be more gassy because the heat from the Sun melts the ice."

"That is super cool!" Lukas exclaims.

The forever calm Freeda resets the GPS again and takes off!

They finally arrive at Pluto. He is holding hands with his moon, Charon.

"Oh boy, he does look very unhappy," says Dr. Dee Dee. "Let's get to work.
We are going to make Pluto heavier and turn up his gravitational force so
he can clear out his orbit and become a planet again!"

Dr. Dee Dee chants with excitement, fingers tingling as she puts on her
gloves and mask:

I'm Dr. Dee Dee Dynamo,
Super Surgeon ON THE GO!
My hands were made to heal.
I cut, I sew, I tie with zeal;
No problem is too big or small,
Dr. Dee Dee Dynamo can tackle them all!

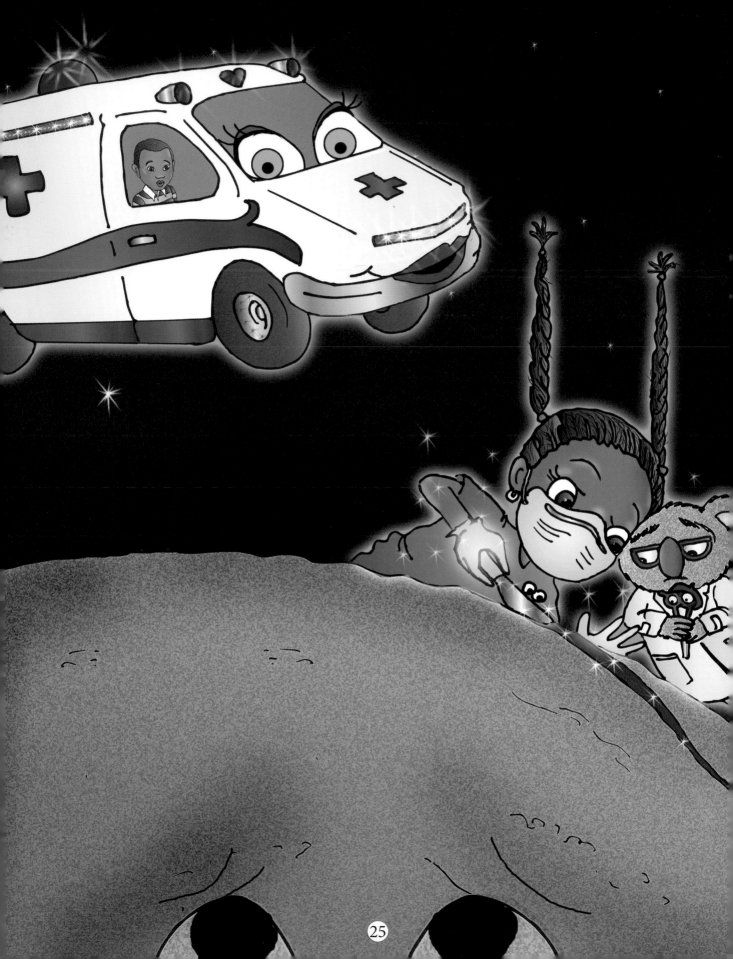

She quickly exits the ambulance and zips towards Pluto.
Kyle follows with Marky.

"Kyle, prepare the work surface," Dr. Dee Dee instructs.

Marky produces the surgical table
and Kyle sets all of the instruments on top.

Dr. Dee Dee prepares the surgical field, holds Slicey Scalpel, who can barely contain himself, and makes a huge incision from the top of Pluto to the bottom. She positions Raoul the Retractor to keep Pluto open.

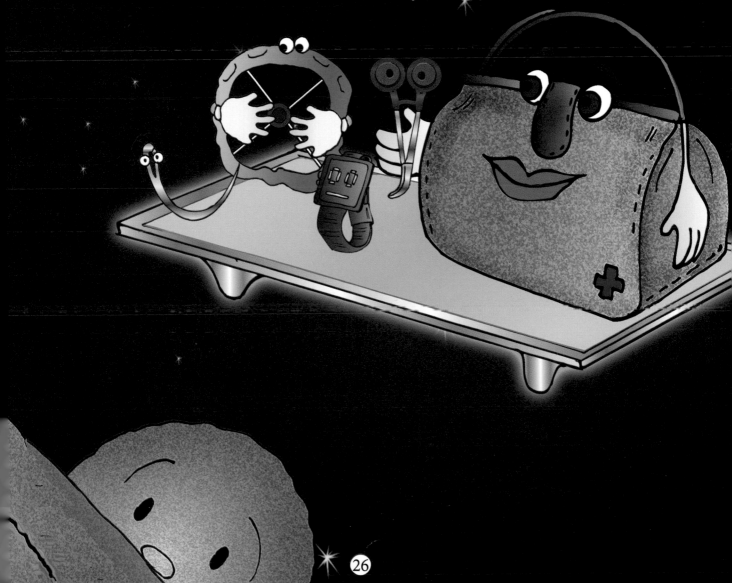

"Come on, Marky, we need to collect lots of rocks and ice to increase Pluto's mass."

The amazing Marky can expand to hold anything. Dr. Dee Dee and Marky jet beyond Pluto to a nearby asteroid belt where they collect thousands of asteroids.

They return to Pluto and empty the asteroids into Pluto's center. Dr. Dee Dee intensely focuses her electrical energy and turns up Pluto's gravitational force.

Nellie Needleholder, Suzy Suture, and Simon Scissors spring into
action. Dr. Dee Dee guides Nellie and Suzy while Kyle follows with Simon.

"Sew, tie, cut... Sew, tie, cut... sew, tie, cut!"
they sing happily until Pluto is completely closed.

She gathers the team, returns to Freeda, and they peer through the window. Pluto is rapidly zipping around his orbit, clearing everything in his path!

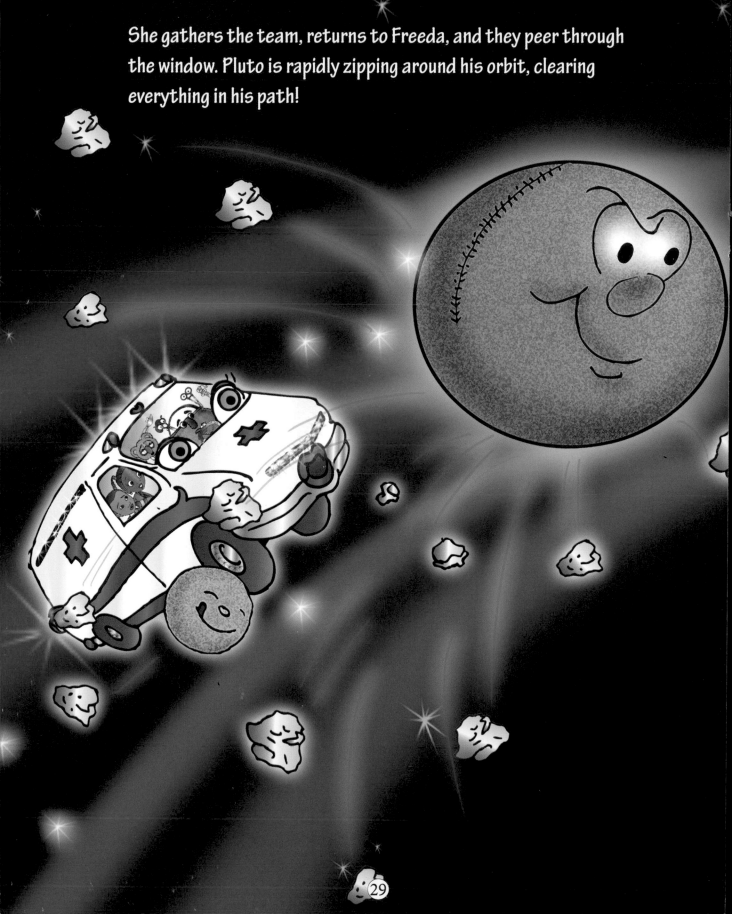

Lukas says, "Wow, Dr. Dee Dee, that is amazing! How..."

"Lukas, please stop asking questions so we can go home," interrupts Kyle irritably.

Freeda jolts and Lukas and the entire team fall over.

"Holymackarolee!" exclaims Lukas. "What in the world?! It feels like we are being sucked towards Pluto!"

"Lukas, you are right!" cries Kyle. "Fasten your seat belts. Pluto's gravitational force is trying to remove us from Pluto's orbit!"

"MISSION ACCOMPLISHED!" says Dr. Dee Dee. "Now Pluto has enough gravitational force to keep his orbit clear and can be upgraded to a planet again."

Dr. Dee Dee checks Wyndee. Thankfully, her trusty watch shows that Dr. Dee Dee has just enough power left to disconnect Freeda from Pluto's gravitational pull.

"Uh oh!" says Lukas. "Something is happening. Pluto seems to be slowing down."

"What's wrong, Pluto?" Dr. Dee Dee asks.

"I thought that being a planet again would make me happy, but clearing my orbit makes me *soooooo* tired," laments Pluto. "I think I will remain a dwarf planet."

Kyle scowls. "Unbelievable!" he grumbles. "All that hard work for nothing!"

"That's not true, Kyle," says Dr. Dee Dee. "Pluto became a planet long enough to now appreciate being a dwarf planet."

"You are right, Dr. Dee Dee!" says Pluto with a huge grin. "Thank you, Dr. Dee Dee Dynamo, SUPER SURGEON ON THE GO!"

"What's going to happen to Pluto's new gravitational force?" inquires Lukas.

"No more questions, Lukas. We are done!" bellows Kyle.

Dr. Dee Dee chuckles, "Gun those engines, Freeda! Let's go home!"

THE END

GLOSSARY

Asteroids: Small rocky or metallic bodies that orbit the Sun.

Dwarf Planets: Bodies that orbit the Sun, are spherical, and are not a moon or satellite of any other planets. They are Ceres, Pluto, Haumea, Makemake, and Eris.

Energy: The capacity or power to do work.

Gravity: The force of attraction between two objects.

Mass: The amount of material in an object.

Milky Way: The galaxy in which the Earth and its Solar system dwell.

Orbit: A path of an object moving around a second object.

Planet: A body that orbits the Sun, is spherical, and can keep its orbit clear of other objects. They are Mercury, Venus, Earth, Mars, Jupiter, Saturn, Uranus, and Neptune.

LEARNING WORDS

Bellows:	a deep, roaring sound
Distress:	extreme pain or suffering
Exuberance:	unrestrained joy
Famished:	extremely hungry
Gullible:	trusting, believes too easily
Lush:	lots of rich, full greenery
Surgeon:	a doctor who treats disease or injuries by operating
Unison:	together
Whisk:	to move quickly
Zeal:	eager, enthusiastic